This book belongs to

W9-BEH-438

tiger tales
an imprint of ME Media, LLC
202 Old Ridgefield Road, Wilton, CT 06897
This paperback edition published 2007
First published in the United States 2003
Originally published in Great Britain 2000
By Little Tiger Press
An imprint of Magi Publications
Text copyright ©2000 Sheridan Cain
Illustrations copyright ©2000 Jack Tickle
ISBN-13: 978-1-58925-403-9
ISBN-10: 1-58925-403-1
Library of Congress Cataloging-in-Publication Data

Cain, Sheridan.
  The crunching munching caterpillar / by Sheridan Cain ;
illustrated by Jack Tickle.
     p. cm.
Summary: Caterpillar wants to fly like Butterfly, Bumblebee,
and Sparrow, and Butterfly thinks his wish may come true.
  ISBN-10 1-58925-025-7 (hardcover)
  ISBN-13 978-1-58925-025-3 (hardcover)
  ISBN-10 1-58925-403-1 (paperback)
  ISBN-13 978-1-58925-403-9 (paperback)
 [1. Caterpillars—Fiction. 2. Butterflies—Fiction. 3.
Flight—Fiction.] I. Tickle, Jack, ill. II. Title.
  PZ7.C1196 Cr 2003
  [E]—dc21
                                    2002014258

Printed in China

For my family
—SC

For Jim and Raechele
—JT

The Crunching Munching Caterpillar

by Sheridan Cain

Illustrated by Jack Tickle

tiger tales

Caterpillar was always hungry. For weeks he crunched and munched his way through the fresh, juicy leaves of a blackberry bush.

Bzzzzzzzzz

One day, Caterpillar was about to
crunch into another leaf when...

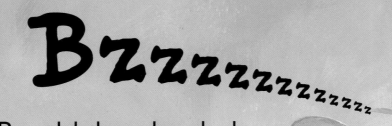

Bumblebee landed
beside him!

"Wow!" said Caterpillar.
"How did you get here?"
"Simple," said Bumblebee.
"I have wings. Look!"
"Oh, I'd like some of
those," said Caterpillar.

Bumblebee flew up into the air and buzzed busily from flower to flower.

Bzzzzz

Bzzzz

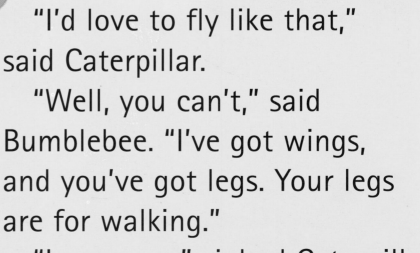

"I'd love to fly like that," said Caterpillar.

"Well, you can't," said Bumblebee. "I've got wings, and you've got legs. Your legs are for walking."

"I guess so," sighed Caterpillar.

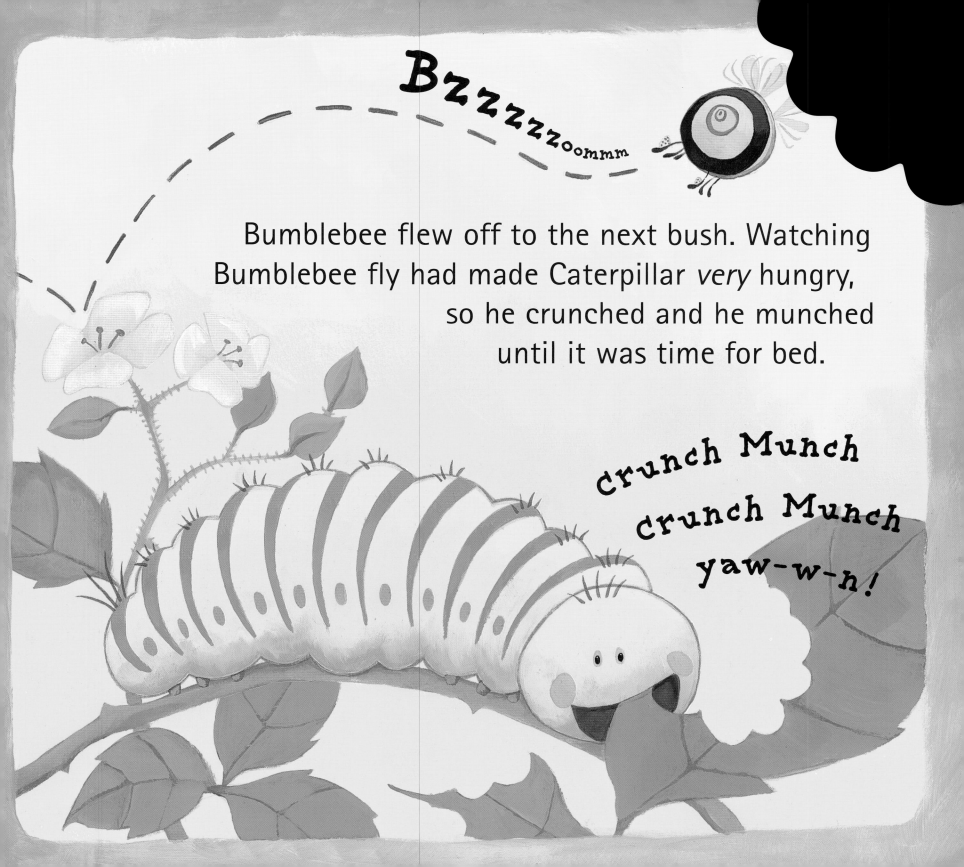

Bzzzzoommm

Bumblebee flew off to the next bush. Watching Bumblebee fly had made Caterpillar *very* hungry, so he crunched and he munched until it was time for bed.

crunch Munch
crunch Munch
yaw-w-n!

Caterpillar woke to the sound of twittering. Birds swooped and soared in the early morning light.

Caterpillar was just about to start his breakfast when...

Sparrow landed
beside him.

"I'd love to fly high in the air like that," said Caterpillar.

"Well, you can't," said Sparrow. "You need to be as light as the dandelion fluff that floats on the breeze. You're far too big to fly. Your legs are for walking."

"I guess so," said Caterpillar sadly.

Caterpillar kept on crunching and munching
all day and into the evening, when the sun
began to set.

crunch
Munch

crunch
Munch

He wrapped a leaf around himself to keep
warm. He was just about to go to sleep when...

Butterfly landed gracefully beside him.

"Oh, I wish I could fly like you," sighed Caterpillar. "But I'm too big and I have legs instead of wings."

Butterfly smiled a secret, knowing smile. "Who knows? Perhaps one day you will fly, light as a feather, like me," she said. "But now, little Caterpillar, you should go to sleep. You look very tired."

Butterfly was right. Caterpillar
suddenly felt very sleepy.
   As Butterfly flew off into the
night sky, he fell into a deep,
deep sleep.

Caterpillar slept all through the winter, and his sleep was filled with dreams.

zzzzzzzzzzz

He dreamed he had wings and was soaring in the blue sky above the tall trees....

He dreamed he was as light as a feather, floating on the breeze.

When Caterpillar woke up he felt the warmth of the spring sun. He was stiff from his long sleep, but he did not feel very hungry. He st r e t c h e d and st r e t c h e d . . .

and a breeze lifted
Caterpillar into the air.

Caterpillar was no longer
short and plump. He had
WINGS! Great, big, wonderful
BUTTERFLY WINGS!

"Wow!" he said. "I'm flying! I'm really flying!"

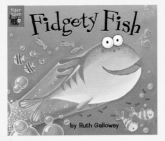

Fidgety Fish
by Ruth Galloway
ISBN-10: 1-58925-377-9
ISBN-13: 978-1-58925-377-3

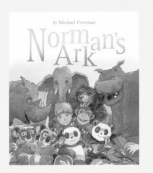

Norman's Ark
by Michael Foreman
ISBN-10: 1-58925-401-5
ISBN-13: 978-1-58925-401-5

Dinosaurs Galore!
by Giles Andreae
Illustrated by David Wojtowycz
ISBN-10: 1-58925-399-X
ISBN-13: 978-1-58925-399-5

Commotion in the Ocean
by Giles Andreae
Illustrated by David Wojtowycz
ISBN-10: 1-58925-366-3
ISBN-13: 978-1-58925-366-7

Explore the world of tiger tales!

More fun-filled and exciting stories await you!
Look for these titles and more at your local library or bookstore.
And have fun reading!

tiger tales

202 Old Ridgefield Road, Wilton, CT 06897

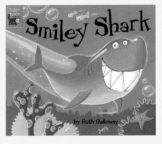

Smiley Shark
by Ruth Galloway
ISBN-10: 1-58925-391-4
ISBN-13: 978-1-58925-391-9

Oops-a-Daisy!
by Claire Freedman
Illustrated by Gaby Hansen
ISBN-10: 1-58925-398-1
ISBN-13: 978-1-58925-398-8

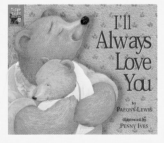

I'll Always Love You
by Paeony Lewis
Illustrated by Penny Ives
ISBN-10: 1-58925-360-4
ISBN-13: 978-1-58925-360-5

Kangaroo Christine
by Guido van Genechten
ISBN-10: 1-58925-396-5
ISBN-13: 978-1-58925-396-4